My Storytime Collection of
★ First Favourite ★ Tales

A catalogue record for this book is available from the British Library

Published by Ladybird Books Ltd
27 Wrights Lane London W8 5TZ
A Penguin Company

© LADYBIRD BOOKS LTD MCMXCIX

Stories in this book were previously published by Ladybird Books Ltd
in the *First Favourite Tales* series.
Chicken Licken illustrations © Sam Childs
LADYBIRD and the device of a Ladybird are trademarks of Ladybird Books Ltd

*All rights reserved. No part of this publication may be reproduced,
stored in a retrieval system, or transmitted in any form or by any means,
electronic, mechanical, photocopying, recording or otherwise,
without the prior consent of the copyright owner.*

My Storytime Collection of
✶ First Favourite ✶ Tales

Ladybird

Introduction

A perfect first collection of timeless and treasured stories, with amusing pictures and lots of funny rhythm and rhyme to delight young children.

Contents

Chicken Licken
based on a traditional folk tale
retold by Mandy Ross
illustrated by Sam Childs

Little Red Riding Hood
based on the story by Jacob and Wilhelm Grimm
retold by Mandy Ross
illustrated by Anja Rieger

The Sly Fox and the Little Red Hen
based on a traditional folk tale
retold by Mandy Ross
illustrated by Marc Chalvin

Jack and the Beanstalk

based on a traditional folk tale
retold by Iona Treahy
illustrated by Ruth Rivers

The Elves and the Shoemaker

based on the story by Jacob and Wilhelm Grimm
retold by Lorna Read
illustrated by Tania Hurt-Newton

Chicken Licken

Chicken Licken is minding his chicken-pecking business one day, when an acorn drops – PLOP! on his head.

"Help!" he cheeps. "The sky is falling down! I'd better go and tell the king."

And off he scurries.

"What's the hurry?" clucks…

…Henny Penny.

"Oh, Henny Penny!" cheeps Chicken Licken. "The sky is falling down! I'm off to tell the king."

"That's not funny!" clucks Henny Penny. "I'd better come, too."

It's a terrible tale!

"Oh, Cocky Locky!" cheeps Chicken Licken. "The sky is falling down! We're off to tell the king."

"What a cock-a-doodle shock!" crows Cocky Locky. "I'd better come, too."

So Chicken Licken, Henny Penny and Cocky Locky scurry along to tell the king.

"Oh, Ducky Lucky and Drakey Lakey!" cheeps Chicken Licken. "The sky is falling down! We're off to tell the king."

"You look very shaky!" quacks Drakey Lakey. "We'd better come, too."

"What's the hurry?" honks...

…Goosey Loosey.

"Oh, Goosey Loosey!" cheeps Chicken Licken. "The sky is falling down! We're off to tell the king."

"Goodness gracious!" gasps Goosey Loosey. "I'd better come, too."

"Oh, Turkey Lurkey!" cheeps Chicken Licken. "The sky is falling down! We're off to tell the king."

"I feel horribly wobbly," gobbles Turkey Lurkey. "I'd better come, too."

So Chicken Licken, Henny Penny, Cocky Locky, Ducky Lucky, Drakey Lakey, Goosey Loosey and Turkey Lurkey scurry along to tell the king.

This way to see the king.

"Oh, Foxy Loxy!" cheeps Chicken Licken. "The sky is falling down! We're off to tell the king."

"Aha!" smiles Foxy Loxy. He has a cunning plan.

"Follow me, my feathery friends," smiles Foxy Loxy. "I can help you find the king."

So Chicken Licken, Henny Penny, Cocky Locky, Ducky Lucky, Drakey Lakey, Goosey Loosey and Turkey Lurkey hurry and scurry behind Foxy Loxy, all the way to…

...the Foxy Loxy Family lair – just in time for dinner.

And that was the end of Chicken Licken, Henny Penny, Cocky Locky, Ducky Lucky, Drakey Lakey, Goosey Loosey and Turkey Lurkey.

And the king never did find out that the sky was falling down.

Little Red Riding Hood

Once upon a time there was a small girl called Little Red Riding Hood. She lived with her parents beside a deep, dark forest.

In a cottage on the other side
of the forest lived her grandmother.

Heh! Heh!

And in the deep, dark forest lived…

...a big, bad wolf.

"Grandmother's poorly," said Little Red Riding Hood's mother one day. "Please take her this cake. But don't stop on the way!"

So Little Red Riding Hood set off through the deep, dark forest. She looked all around.

There wasn't a sound.

Then who should she meet but…

…the big, bad wolf.

"Good day, my dear," growled the wolf with a big, bad smile. "What are you doing here?"

She looks delicious!

"I'm going to Grandmother's to take her a cake," replied Little Red Riding Hood.

What big teeth!

The wolf had a plan.

"Wouldn't your grandmother like some of these flowers?" he smiled.

"What a good idea," said Little Red Riding Hood. And she stopped to pick a big bunch.

Meanwhile, the wolf sped ahead through the deep, dark forest. At last he arrived at…

...Grandmother's cottage.

"I'm HUNGRY," thought the big, bad wolf, licking his lips. And he knock-knock-knocked at the door.

"Hello, Grandmother," growled the wolf. "It's Little Red Riding Hood."

"That sounds more like the big, bad wolf," thought Grandmother, and she crept quickly under the bed.

The wolf went in. He looked all around, but there wasn't a sound.

Then his tummy rumbled.

"No one's here," he grumbled. "Never mind. Little Red Riding Hood will be along soon."

It's dusty! I mustn't sneeze.

Quickly the wolf put on Grandmother's dressing gown and nightcap. Then he hopped into bed and pretended to nap.

"Heh! Heh! Heh!" he snarled. "Little Red Riding Hood will never know it's me!"

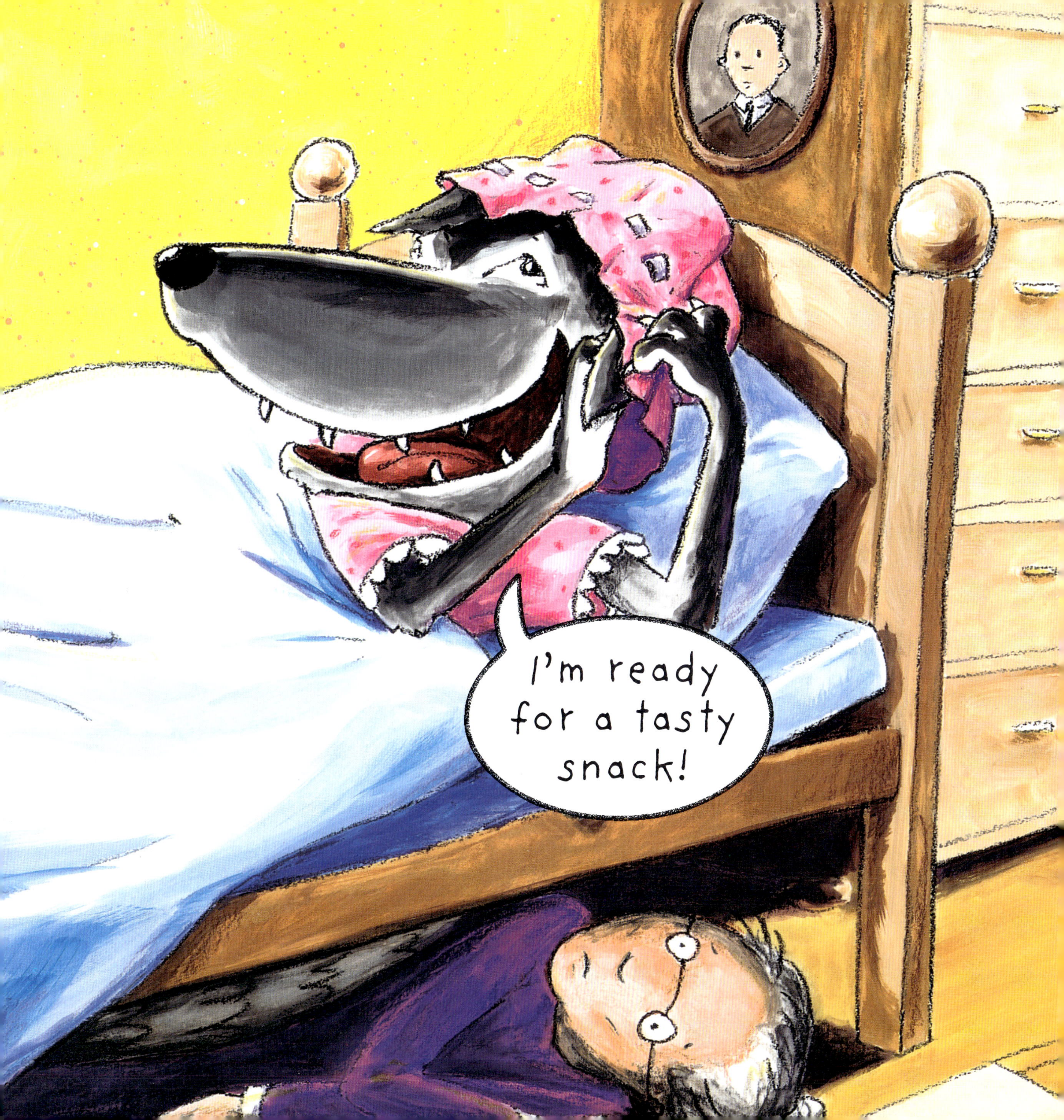
I'm ready for a tasty snack!

Soon Little Red Riding Hood knock-knock-knocked at the door.

"Hello, Grandmother," she called. "It's Little Red Riding Hood."

"Come in, my dear," growled the wolf.

Little Red Riding Hood opened the door.

"Oh, Grandmother!" she gasped…

"…What big ears you have!"

"All the better to hear you with, my dear," growled the wolf.

"And Grandmother, what big eyes you have!"

"All the better to see you with, my dear," growled the wolf.

"And Grandmother, what big teeth you have!"

"All the better to…

Those teeth remind me of someone.

"...GOBBLE YOU UP!" roared the wolf.

But as he leapt out of bed, Grandmother's nightcap flopped right over his head.

I can't see anything!

"Quick! Down here, dear!" whispered Grandmother, and she pulled Little Red Riding Hood under the bed.

Just then, a woodcutter passed by the cottage.
He heard a growling and howling…

and he dashed inside.
With one *SWISH!* of his axe he killed
the big, bad wolf.

The woodcutter looked all around. But there wasn't a sound. And then…

…out crept Little Red Riding Hood and Grandmother from under the bed.

And Little Red Riding Hood said, "Mother was right. I'll *never* stop again on my way through the forest!"

The Sly Fox
and the
Little Red Hen

Once there was a little red hen. She lived in a little red henhouse, safe and sound, with a little blue door and windows all around.

Peck, peck, peck!

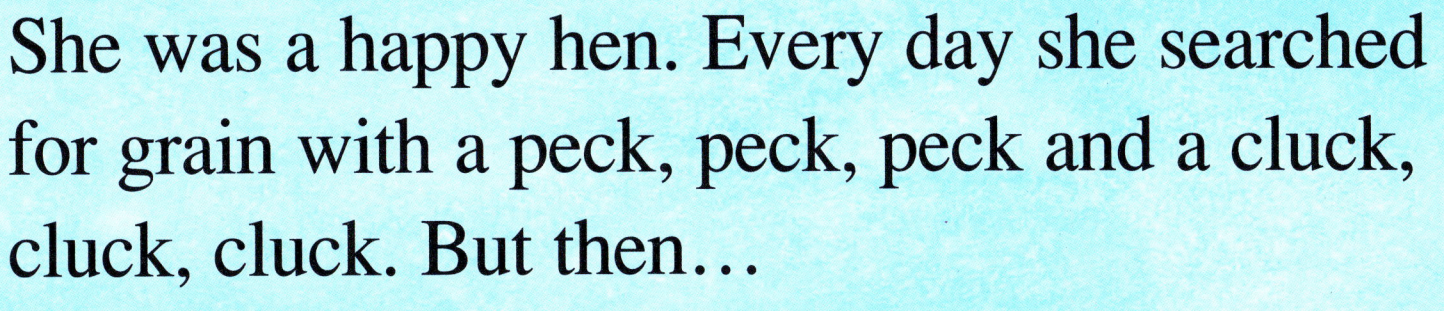

She was a happy hen. Every day she searched for grain with a peck, peck, peck and a cluck, cluck, cluck. But then…

...a sly young fox and his mother moved into a nearby den.

The sly fox was always hungry. He licked his lips when he saw the little red hen searching for grain with a peck, peck, peck and a cluck, cluck, cluck.
And then…

...the sly fox tried to catch the little red hen. He plotted and planned, again and again.

I'm hungry for that hen.

But the little red hen was clever. She always got away, with a peck, peck, peck and a cluck, cluck, cluck. But then…

…the sly fox thought up a very sly plan.

"Mother, boil some water in a pan," he said. "I'll bring home supper tonight."

Then he crept over to the little red henhouse.
And he waited…

…until at last the little red hen came out to search for grain with a peck, peck, peck and a cluck, cluck, cluck.

Quick as a flash, the sly fox slipped into the henhouse. And he waited...

…until the little red hen came hurrying home.

As soon as she saw the fox, she flew up to the rafters.

"You can't catch me now!" she laughed, with a peck, peck, peck and a cluck, cluck, cluck.

"All part of my plan," smiled the fox on the ground. And slowly he started to chase his tail, round and round…

…and round and round, faster and faster…

until the little red hen up in the rafters grew dizzy.

"Oh!" she clucked. "My poor head's spinning. I'm all in a tizzy." And she dropped down – plop! – straight into the fox's sack.

"Ha!" laughed the fox. And then…

Got her!

...the fox slung the sack over his shoulder and set off for home with the little red hen.

After a while, he stopped for a rest. The sun was warm and soon he was snoozing.

"Now's my chance," whispered the little red hen, and out she crept *without* a peck, peck, peck or a cluck, cluck, cluck.

Quickly she rolled some large stones into the sack and tied a knot at the top.

Then she ran all the way home and didn't stop till she was safe in her little red henhouse.

The fox woke up and went on his way, hungry for his supper.

My tummy's rumbling!

"This hen is heavy!" he said to himself, licking his lips. "She'll make a good meal."

"Is the pot boiling, Mother?" he called at the den. "Look who I've got! It's the little red hen."

"Throw her in, son," said his mother. "She'll make a nice snack."

So the sly fox opened up the sack. Into the boiling water crashed the stones with a SPLASH!

And that was the end of the sly fox and his mother.

Cluck, cluck, cluck!

And the little red hen lived happily ever after in her little red henhouse, searching for grain with a peck, peck, peck and a cluck, cluck, cluck.

Jack and the Beanstalk

Once there was a boy called Jack who lived with his mother. They were so poor that she said to him one day, "We'll have to sell our cow – it's the only way."

So Jack took the cow to market.

"I'll miss you, Daisy."

On the way, Jack met a stranger.

"I'll give you five beans for that cow," she said. "They're magic beans…"

"Done!" said Jack. But when he got back…

"Five beans for our cow?" cried his mother. And she threw them out of the window.

All through the night, a beanstalk grew… and grew… till it was right out of sight.

Before his mother could say a word, Jack climbed… and climbed… and he didn't stop till he reached…

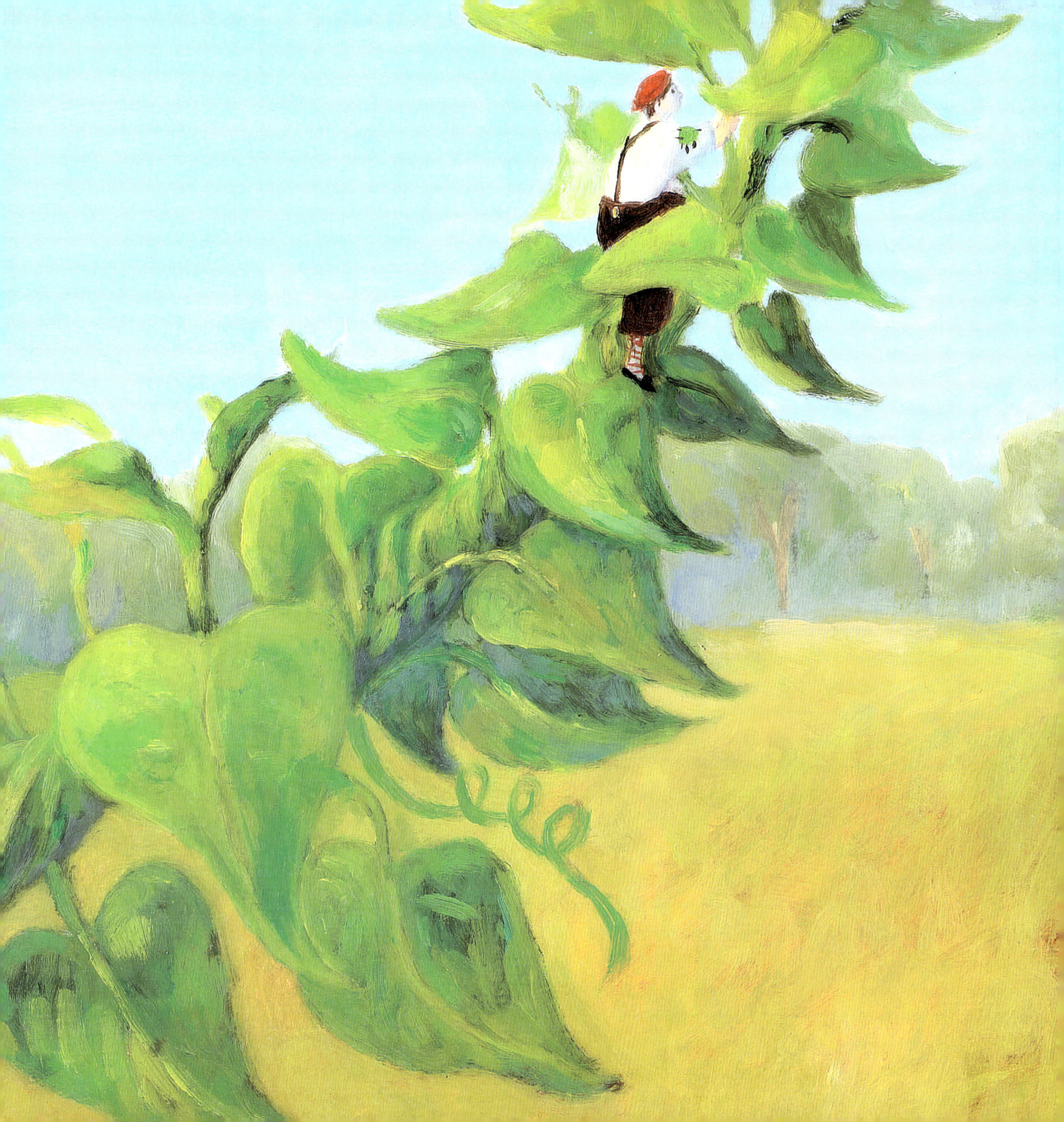

…the top. There Jack saw a giant castle. He knock-knock-knocked, and a giantess opened the door.

Inside, Jack could hear a **thumping** and a **banging** and a **stamping** and a **crashing**!

What a noise!

"Quick," said the giantess. "Hide! My husband is hungry!"

"Fee, fi, fo fum! Watch out everyone, HERE I COME!" roared the giant.

The giant sat down for his supper. He ate a hundred boiled potatoes, and a hundred chocolate biscuits. And then, feeling a bit happier, he got out his gold.

The giant started counting his coins,
but soon... he was snoozing.

Zzzzzz...

Jack snatched the gold and *raced* down the beanstalk.

"Gold!" cried Jack's mother when she saw what he'd got. "We're not poor any more!"

But Jack wanted to go back up the beanstalk. The next day he climbed… and climbed… and he didn't stop till he reached the top.

Inside the castle, Jack hid when he heard…

It's you again!

a **thumping** and a **banging** and a **stamping** and a **crashing**.

"Fee, fi, fo, fum!
Watch out everyone,
HERE I COME!" roared the giant.

The giant sat down for his supper. He ate two hundred baked potatoes, and two hundred jellies. And then, feeling a bit happier, he got out his hen that laid golden eggs.

The hen started laying, but soon… the giant was snoozing. Jack snatched the hen and *raced* down the beanstalk.

"Golden eggs from a golden hen!" cried Jack's mother. "Now we'll never be poor again!"

The next day, Jack climbed the beanstalk once more.

"Fee, fi, fo, fum!
Watch out everyone,
HERE I COME!" roared the giant.

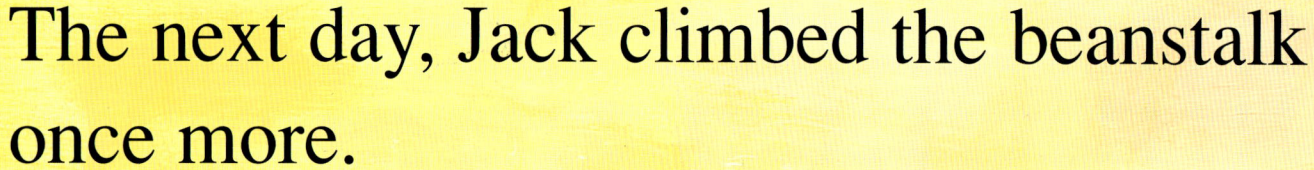

The giant sat down for his supper. He ate three hundred roast potatoes, and three hundred cream cakes. And then, feeling a bit happier, he got out his silver harp.

The harp sang him lullabies, and soon… the giant was snoozing. Jack snatched the harp and *raced* down the beanstalk.

But the harp called out, "Master! Master!"

The giant woke up and started to chase after Jack.

"Bring the axe, Mother!" shouted Jack as he neared the ground. Then he chopped and he chopped and didn't stop till… CRASH! Down came the beanstalk and the giant.

And with the gold and the harp and the eggs and the hen, Jack and his mother were never poor again.

The Elves and the Shoemaker

Late one night a shoemaker sat
cutting his leather with a snip, snip, snap,
watched by his wife and watched by his cat.

"I'll sew them tomorrow," the shoemaker said. He went to bed hungry. There was no bread. The cupboard was bare. Nothing there…

"No supper tonight?"

In the morning when he opened his eyes, there on the bench was a big surprise. Someone had stitched the shoes. But who?

The shoemaker blinked and scratched his head. "What teeny, tiny stitches!" he said. "Who could do a thing like that?"

"Not me," miaowed the cat.

He sold the shoes for a very good price,
and bought more leather, and meat and rice.
They had a good supper that night.

Then he cut the leather with a snip, snip, snap.
"I'm ever so tired," he said to the cat.
"I can't stop yawning.
I'll stitch these in the morning."

Time for bed!

In the morning when he opened his eyes, there on the bench was a bigger surprise. *Four* pairs of shoes had been stitched in the night!

What purr-fect shoes!

The shoemaker blinked and scratched his head.
"What teeny, tiny stitches!" he said.
"Who could do a thing like that?"

"Not me," miaowed the cat.

Customers came to the shop in queues
when they heard about the beautiful shoes.
They tried them on…
Soon they were all gone!

And now with all the money he'd made, the shoemaker went to the market and paid for leather in blue and green and red.

He cut the leather with a snip, snip, snap, watched by his wife and watched by his cat. His wife said, "Now we'll see what happens to that!"

Next morning when they got out of bed,
they found shoes in blue and green and red.

"Such teeny, tiny stitches!" the shoemaker said.

I like the blue shoes!

From far away, when they heard the news, people came to the shop in queues.

"What beautiful shoes!" they cried.
"It's hard to choose!"

The shoemaker sat and counted his money.
He thought, "Isn't it funny! I'm suddenly rich,
and I haven't even sewn a stitch!"

The shoemaker's wife said, "We have to find whoever it is who's being so kind. Let's watch in your workshop tonight."

Eek!

So they left a candle burning bright
and there they hid in the dead of night.
Midnight chimed... the door went *creak*...

…and three little elves came skippy-skip in,
with silver tools in a teeny, tiny tin,
but their clothes were threadbare and thin.

Tip, tip, tap!

Their silver hammers went tip, tip, tap, and they cut and sewed with a snip, snip, snap, and the shoes were made in a flash.

Snip, snip, snap!

When the elves had left, the shoemaker's wife said, "I've never seen, in all my life, three little elves, so threadbare –
I'll sew them all new clothes to wear!"

Where's my thimble?

She sewed a tiny dress and tiny jackets
and tiny tartan trousers with pockets—
and the shoemaker made tiny, beautiful boots.

The very next night, they left the clothes there on the bench in three neat rows. Then they hid themselves to watch for the elves.

When the elves found the suits and the tiny boots, they put them on and danced through the door singing, "Shoes we'll make here no more!"

They've never seen another elf.
The shoemaker stitches his shoes himself.
But every day he's grateful for the dinner on his table.

And every night to the window he creeps
(for he made a promise that still he keeps.)

"Thank you, elves," he whispers…
and then he sleeps.

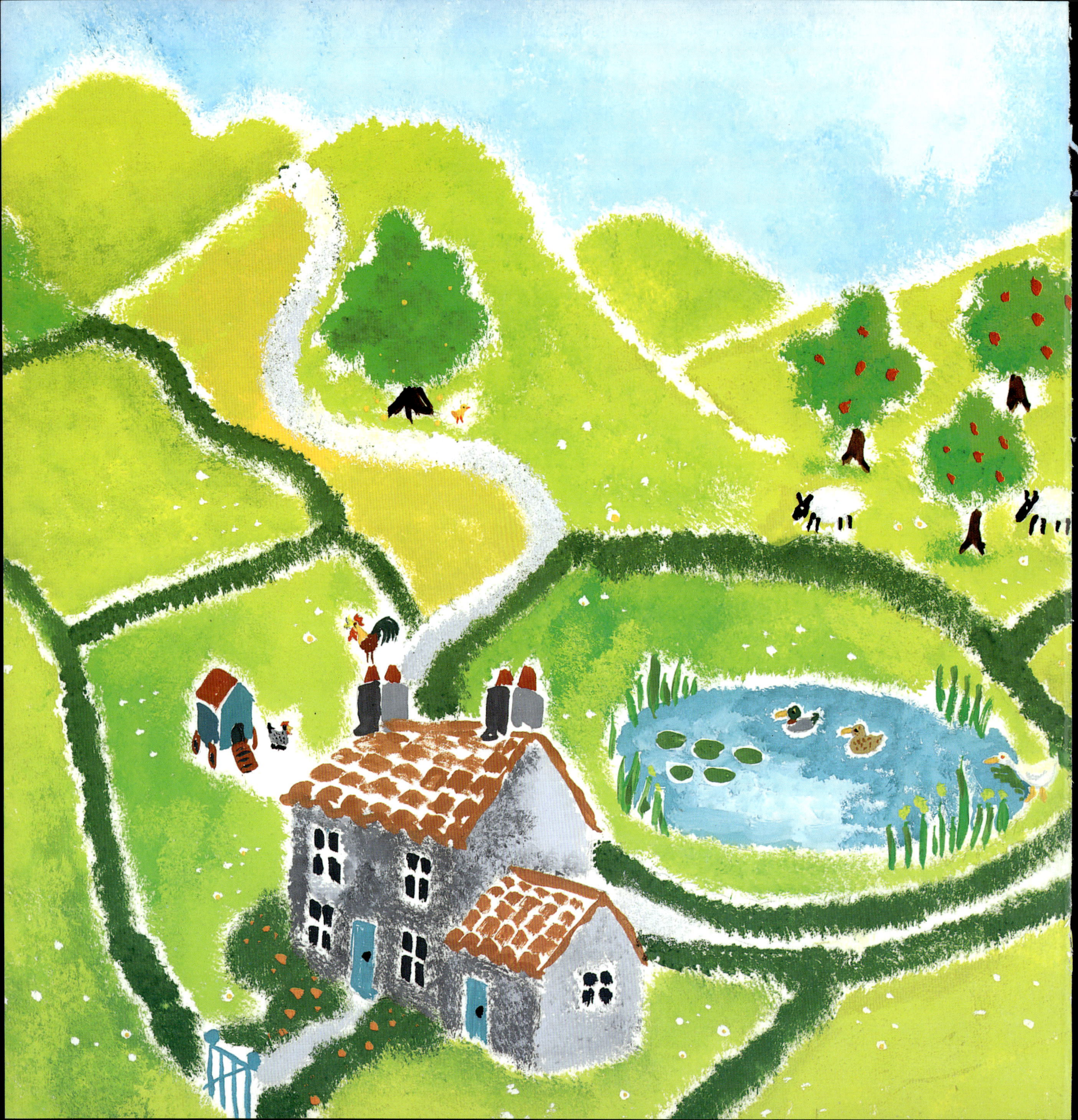